INDIGO

INDIGO

ALICE HOFFMAN

scholastic press ⟐ new york

Copyright © 2002 by Alice Hoffman

All rights reserved. Published by Scholastic Press, a division of Scholastic Inc.,
Publishers since 1920. SCHOLASTIC and SCHOLASTIC PRESS
and associated logos are trademarks and/or registered trademarks
of Scholastic Inc.

No part of this publication may be reproduced, or stored in a retrieval system,
or transmitted in any form or by any means, electronic, mechanical,
photocopying, recording, or otherwise, without written permission of the publisher.
For information regarding permission, write to Scholastic Inc., Attention:
Permissions Department, 555 Broadway, New York, NY 10012.

LIBRARY OF CONGRESS CATALOG-IN-PUBLICATION DATA
Hoffman, Alice.
Indigo / by Alice Hoffman.
p. cm.
Summary: When her mother dies Martha is so unhappy living in
the dried-up town of Oak Grove, that she convinces two unusual brothers
who long to return to the ocean to run away with her.
ISBN 0-439-25635-6
[1. Friendship—Fiction. 2. Runaways—Fiction.
3. Self-perception—Fiction.] I. Title.
PZ7.H67445 In 2002

[Fic]—dc21	2001042617
10 9 8 7 6 5 4 3 2 1	02 03 04 05 06

The text type was set in Adobe Garamond.
Book design by Elizabeth B. Parisi

Printed in the United States of America
First edition, April 2002

To those born under the signs of water,

especially to wolfe Martin.

with gratitude and love to Jean Feiwel

and Elizabeth Szabla,

for wisdom, generosity, and heart.

Thanks also to Jennifer Braunstein,

Elizabeth Eulberg, Erica o'Rourke,

and a special debt of gratitude to Elizabeth Parisi

for design that is a mermaid's dream.

INDIGO

chapter
one

The town of Oak Grove was so far away from the ocean that most people who lived there had never seen a seagull or listened to the whisper of a pink shell. They certainly hadn't heard the way the sea can call to you on a hot July day when wave after wave beckons and the water is endless and clear.

As a matter of fact, people in Oak Grove dreaded water. This was a town with a history of terrible flooding. Fifteen years earlier, the spring that fed Penman's Creek overflowed, leaving Oak Grove awash so that people had to clamor onto their roofs. When the floodwaters finally receded, the creek was dammed up, and folks went overboard to protect Oak Grove. The town council ordered the public swimming pool drained; lawn watering was limited to an hour a day, showers to ten minutes long. Drier was better in Oak Grove, or so people said. And the weather appeared to cooperate. The only thing that seemed endless here was the perfect blue sky that was the same day after day, without the slightest hint of rain or the hope of a stray cloud passing by.

Most residents of Oak Grove were grateful for its climate. But not Martha Glimmer. As far as Martha was concerned, this was the worst year of her life. Martha hated Oak Grove, where there was nothing better to do on a brilliant spring day than sit on the roof of her father's garage with her two best friends, Trevor and Eli McGill, and throw rocks at the line of tin cans they'd arranged down below.

Martha hated the fact that it never rained in Oak Grove; she hated the way the grass grew so dry, it creaked when you walked on it; and she hated Hildy Swoon, a neighbor who brought casseroles over almost every night and tried to convince Martha's father that he should start a new life. Most of all, Martha hated people who pitied a girl like herself, who'd lost her mother the year before, at such a tender age. While Martha was at it, she hated being thirteen, a number that was clearly unlucky, at least for her, for this was the year when she'd grown seven inches; her legs were now so long and gawky, she often tripped over her own feet.

Martha's friend, Trevor McGill, completely disagreed; he enjoyed being thirteen. He had grown taller as well, one of the few boys their age who was the same height as Martha. But whereas Martha was uncomfortable with her size, Trevor couldn't be happier with his. As for Trevor's brother, Eli, at eleven, he was at an age when anything older was preferable, and could hardly wait to grow up.

Both the McGill brothers had dark hair and sea-green eyes, and they certainly weren't like anyone else in town. It wasn't anything obvious that set the boys apart, but when you considered some of their odder traits, the little things added up. From the time the boys were toddlers there had been gossip about them. Susie Lawrence, who worked at the Sweet Shoppe, confided that the boys threw away any candy their mother bought them, tossing out jelly beans and chocolate bars alike, and that wasn't very normal, was it? Their old baby-sitter, Gretchen Hardy, whispered that Trevor and Eli had refused to nap unless she brought them into the kitchen. They'd cry and bellow like walruses until Gretchen turned on the tap full blast, and then, instantly, the sound of running water lulled them to sleep.

As the boys grew older, they grew stranger as well, or so people said, especially those folks who enjoyed gossip far more than they enjoyed their neighbors' good fortune. But who could blame people for discussing how odd it was that Eli McGill had been found splashing around in a bathtub — thankfully, with all his clothes on — at Annamaria Chamberlain's tenth birthday party while everyone else devoured cake and ice cream. Or how unnerving it was when Trevor fixed people with his pale green eyes, staring until even the most landlocked citizens found themselves dreaming of running off to sea with the wind at their backs and everything else in their lives just a memory.

Most of Oak Grove had noticed that the brothers seemed to live on a diet of fish, preferring tuna and sardines to pizza and burgers. Those who were closest to the boys' parents, Charlie and Kate McGill, admitted they'd been startled to see Trevor and Eli add handfuls of salt to their drinking water and then swallow it down without a burp, as if the briny mixture had come from a clear mountain spring.

And so it was understandable that people in Oak Grove were wary of the McGill boys, but in the most polite and orderly way. This was a town where everything was orderly, after all, another thing Martha Glimmer hated about it. Streets crisscrossed at perfect right angles; houses had to be painted white by decree of the town council; children went to the same school their parents had attended, and were as predictable and reliable as their forefathers, the ones who'd taught their sons and daughters to follow the rules instead of their hearts.

It was following his heart that had led Eli McGill to free the frogs in the science lab, even though the science teacher chased him all the way to the dried-out creek bed. But Eli was so fast, he couldn't be caught. The children of Oak Grove called him "Eel" after that, and they dubbed his brother "Trout," because of the older boy's green eyes that never seemed to blink and the gasping look he had whenever someone was being bullied in the school yard, as if someone else's pain caused him heartache as well.

Perhaps these nicknames stuck because of the characteristic most people considered strangest of all about the brothers. Although it had never bothered Martha Glimmer one bit, most folks in town found something else about Trout and Eel particularly alarming: The boys had a thin webbing between their fingers and toes.

Dr. Marsh, who'd been Oak Grove's physician for a good thirty years and who was rarely flustered, blinked when the young McGill boys were brought in for their first visit after they'd been adopted. When he saw the webbing he gulped like a fish himself and admitted he'd never seen anything like it before. But they were good, healthy boys, and Dr. Marsh patted their sleek heads and told Kate and Charlie McGill that, given all the things that could go wrong in this world, a meshing of skin between a child's fingers and toes was nothing to worry about. In time, it would probably wear away.

But now that the boys were thirteen and eleven it was clear the trait was permanent, and although this made certain activities difficult — a proper baseball mitt was impossible to find, and bowling was out of the question — Eel's fingers could spread so wide, he could play a duet on the piano all by himself, and Trout could palm a basketball with no trouble at all.

The brothers' unusual taste in food never diminished, but that was easily accommodated as well. When Jeanette Morton, who owned the bakery, realized the boys preferred anchovy pies to chocolate cakes, she happily perfected a crust so flaky, and a filling so rich, that even Mr. McGill, who'd always loved sweets, grew to prefer anchovy pie to apple or blueberry. Martha's father, who owned the grocery, ordered fresh tuna each week, which Mrs. McGill served raw for the boys and lightly broiled for herself and her husband. As for all the salt the brothers consumed, well, their mother told people such a preference was probably caused by a vitamin deficiency.

By now Martha Glimmer barely noticed anything unusual about her two friends. Some people say "live and let live," and that was the group Martha belonged to. A real friend believes in you when you don't believe in yourself, and this had always been true for Martha and the boys, especially when Martha's mother fell ill. But there will always be those who zero in on anything different and turn such habits and traits into ammunition — Richard Grady, for instance, their classmate who called Trout "flipper boy" and asked Eel right to his face how it felt to look like a water snake.

Martha Glimmer wasn't interested in the opinions of Richard Grady or of anyone else in

Oak Grove. She wasn't planning on staying in this boring town one second longer than necessary. She wanted to go to New York and San Francisco and Paris, cities where her mother had lived before she'd come to Oak Grove and married Martha's father, before she opened the dancing school over on Main Street, right above the bakery, where the aroma of chocolate and vanilla bean wafted up through the ceiling, so that children who took lessons there always seemed sweeter following an hour of stretches and pliés or an afternoon spent learning the rudiments of the tango.

After Martha's mother had passed on last year, Hildy Swoon began bringing over her casseroles. She fixed terrible tasting concoctions made out of rice and peas, canned soup and potatoes, but Martha's father was so heartbroken, he didn't seem to notice how awful the food was.

From the start, Hildy Swoon made it clear that she wasn't interested in Martha's company. When she stayed for dinner, Hildy informed Martha that she preferred children to eat in the kitchen rather than the dining room to ensure that the adults wouldn't be disturbed. Although Mr. Glimmer seemed grateful for the help around the house, he didn't notice that Hildy didn't seem to like much about Martha, and she certainly didn't like the McGill brothers. Whenever she was visiting and the boys came to call, Hildy made a clicking, disapproving sound, like a hen that can't get comfortable on her nest.

"Those boys are much too strange," Hildy

told Martha and her father. "There is definitely something fishy about them."

In Martha's opinion some people were meant to be mothers, and some people, such as Hildy Swoon, were not. You could easily tell who was who by whether or not they listened to you. Hildy Swoon always hummed when Martha spoke and then she said, "What?" when it was perfectly clear she hadn't listened to a word and couldn't care less about what Martha thought. Kate McGill, on the other hand, was clearly meant to be somebody's mother. She stopped what she was doing whenever her boys came rushing into the house. One look and anyone could tell her happiness could be measured in direct proportion to the happiness of her sons.

Each spring, Mrs. McGill celebrated the anniversary of the day when she and her husband had adopted the boys. Charlie McGill had closed down his construction company and they'd gone on vacation to Ocean City, expecting to bring home nothing more than seashells and sand in their shoes. Instead, they'd returned to Oak Grove with the two boys, and from then on Kate McGill had been the happiest woman in town.

Martha Glimmer felt welcome at the McGills' night or day. There were always plates of seaweed cakes, which tasted far better than they sounded, and fish soup simmering on the stove. At the Glimmers' the only place Martha and her friends felt comfortable was up on the roof of the garage now that Hildy was so often around, mopping the floors with ammonia and straightening out the dresser drawers. The friends spent most afternoons with nothing better to do but knock down the cans they had placed in a line down below in the grass.

"You are so lucky," Martha told Trout and Eel. "You have such a great family."

Her own father had gotten sadder with each day of Martha's mother's illness. By the time Hildy started to call, he didn't seem like himself anymore. The man he used to be would have never let Hildy Swoon take over their house. He would have never been too grief-stricken to notice that his daughter left the room every time Hildy walked in.

"Lucky?" Trout held up a webbed hand.

"That's nothing," Martha insisted. "That's

not the only thing people should see when they look at you."

Trout had no idea how handsome he was. He didn't care about such things. He concentrated on knocking down more cans than his brother did before giving Martha her turn. One day, Martha might be a dancer in New York City or Paris and Trout might fall in love with her, but for now they were both thirteen and she beat him and Eel at their game, knocking down ten cans in a row.

"Now, that's luck," Trout teased.

Martha made a face at him, but she knew that Trout was always glad when she won. This was one more reason why she didn't care if he was different. What mattered was that Trout McGill was the one person aside from her

mother who believed that Martha would someday leave Oak Grove, and that no matter how
tall she was, or how uncomfortable with herself,
she would be a dancer. He believed in dreams,
in the endings that people told you could never
happen, in disappointments reversed and luck
that lasted.

Perhaps this was because Trout's own dream
was a simple one. He wanted to see the ocean.

Trout was the sort of person who could be
talking to you and daydreaming at the same
time and you wouldn't even know it, except that
every now and then he'd murmur *tide* or *starfish*
when a simple *yes* or *no* would have done. Again
and again he'd asked his parents to take him to
the shore, but each time he had, Kate McGill
had gotten a worried look and Charlie McGill

would start planning a vacation that would take them hiking high up into the mountains.

"You used to go to Ocean City every year. I've seen the photographs," Trout would say. "I'm thirteen and I've never even been to the beach."

"I'm eleven and I've never collected seashells," Eel would add, although he had a conch shell, which he'd taken from the science lab, that he kept hidden under his bed. When he held the shell to his ear the lullaby of the waves inside helped him fall asleep.

One weekend Trout and Eel decided to paint their bedroom blue. The walls were the turquoise of the southern seas, the ceiling was cobalt, the floors indigo, the color of waters so deep and distant, no human had ever seen them before. Here in this room anyone could imagine the sound of waves breaking. Even Martha swore she could hear seagulls and smell the salt-air.

It was a wonderful room, but Charlie McGill was not pleased when he opened the door and saw all that endless blue.

"If you knew what the ocean was like, you'd be grateful to live in a place as dry as Oak Grove," Charlie told his boys. "Water is dangerous, and that's always been true. Before the town ordered Penman's Creek drained and hired me to build the flood wall, we had a terrible time whenever a storm came through. People lost everything. Be glad you're here in Oak Grove, high and dry."

A few days later, when the boys got home from school, they found their room had been painted white. Gone were the southern seas and the farthest waters. Even Eel's seashell had disappeared, and he wondered how he would ever manage to get to sleep.

When Kate McGill saw the hurt expressions on the boys' faces, she tried to explain. "You have to understand your father lived through the worst flood in Oak Grove's history. And then he had a terrible experience one year when we were on vacation in Ocean City. He tried to rescue someone from drowning, but it was too late. Ever since, he's been hydrophobic."

Trout looked up *hydrophobia* in the dictionary. Charlie McGill was a kind and generous man, but he was definitely hydrophobic — which was defined as a fear of water. As a matter of fact, Charlie's construction company specialized in tearing out bathtubs and replacing them with shower stalls. The less water the better, as far as he was concerned. Everyone knew Charlie would have worked for free building the wall of rocks that dammed up Penman's Creek if the town hadn't hired him for the job. Of course a man like that could not abide a room that was as blue as the sea.

"I can't believe your father did this," Martha said when she saw the white room. She knew how much work the brothers had put into all that blue, and it wasn't fair for the room to be returned to the way it had been before their effort. It wasn't right to have someone charge into your world without even asking, acting as if you were nothing more than an egg to be flipped and flopped, sunny-side up or scrambled, depending on the whims of whoever ran your life.

Hildy Swoon, for instance, had let herself into the Glimmers' house one day when no one was home. She had taken all of Martha's mother's clothes from the hall closet, packed them in boxes, and stored them in the attic without even asking. Martha had gone upstairs and retrieved her mother's yellow shawl, the one with the fringe and the embroidered poppies that made Martha feel as though she could travel through time whenever it was wrapped around her shoulders. Martha rarely danced anymore, except when she wore the shawl. Then she could close her eyes and imagine she was back at the dance studio, which was now used as the bakery's storeroom. She could smell sugar and hear her mother's voice. She could dance like an angel, even though she was much too tall.

It was not long after the boys' room was repainted that Martha came home to find the shawl missing. She looked through her bureau, through her closet, even under her bed, but there was no mistake about it, the shawl was gone. Martha ran to the basement and there it was, hanging on a clothesline, shrunken and discolored. Hildy came up behind her.

"I decided to wash that dirty old thing," Hildy Swoon informed Martha. "But it wasn't very well made."

"It was silk." Martha did her best not to let

Hildy see her cry. "It wasn't supposed to be washed like a rag."

"Well, that's what it is now," Hildy replied. "But at least it's clean."

Martha took the shawl, folded it carefully, and put it into her backpack, where it would be safe from Hildy. That evening she went over to the McGills', where she found the boys sitting on the roof of their own garage since they no longer felt comfortable in their white room. Martha climbed up the ladder and sat in between the brothers. Together they dreamed of starting new lives. They'd live by the ocean, they'd visit New York City, they'd paint every room in their house blue, then swim and dance beneath the constellations each night.

"But we're trapped here," Martha moaned.

"High and dry," Trout said moodily, his eyes flashing the color of the sea during a storm.

"Not necessarily," Eel said.

Eel didn't believe anything should be trapped, not frogs, not fish, and certainly not people. He was fearless and smart and he didn't speak much, unless he had something worth saying. At such times, Eel would speak his mind no matter the consequences.

"There's nobody who could stop us if we decided to leave. It's the only way we'll ever get to see the ocean," Eel declared.

Martha and Trout looked at each other. The lilacs were blooming as best they could in a town that was so dry, even the stars looked dusty up in the sky. Eel's idea passed between

Martha and Trout like a blue wave. Sometimes words spoken are the ones you've been afraid to think, but once they're said aloud there's no way to make them disappear. There, on a clear evening, in a town where it seemed nothing ever happened and nothing ever changed, these three friends decided to take hold of their fate.

chapter
TWO

At midnight the wind in the trees can sound like the ocean. The moonlight can make a road appear as endless as the sea. Martha noticed this as she climbed out her window, stopping to tack a note for her father on the door before she headed to meet the McGills. She had her backpack in which she had stowed crackers and peanut butter for herself, sardines for the boys, along with a change of clothes and her mother's yellow shawl.

Being out so late reminded Martha of the way her mother sometimes would wake her unexpectedly to bring her out onto the lawn to dance beneath the stars. Standing in the dark and thinking about her mother and the way she would laugh as they sneaked out of the house, as if they shared the best secret in the world, did something strange to Martha. Her mother suddenly seemed present in some deep way. Martha didn't know if she could take another step. But then she heard Trout whistle, and she started running. Before she knew it, she was halfway down the road, to the place where Trout and Eel were waiting beside the mailbox that Hildy Swoon had cleaned with a stiff metal brush to get rid of every bit of dust and grime.

"We have a compass and thirty-five dollars," Eel told Martha as they started down the road. "We charted the route to Ocean City, and if we walk eight hours a day we'll be there in ten days."

"Ten days?" Martha was surprised. "I only brought enough food for one night."

"You don't have to go." Trout didn't look at Martha as he spoke. She knew he was giving her the chance to change her mind.

"Of course I do." Martha wasn't about to lose her best friends. If they were gone, there would be no one to talk to. No one to trust. "You'd be lost without me," she said.

People went searching for their dreams all the time, didn't they? Still, Martha dragged behind the boys in the moonlight. She was thinking about how sad her father was and how he would feel when he went to wake her for school and discovered she was gone. All he would find was her open window, along with the note on the door. *I'm sorry,* she'd written. *I love you, but I don't feel I belong here anymore.*

"Race you to the town line," Eel called.

The friends ran as fast as they could, with Eel, always the fastest, out in front. They raced down Main Street, past the shuttered grocery that Martha's father owned, past the bakery and what was once the dance studio, past Charlie McGill's construction company. They turned onto Elm and ran along the dried-out bed of Penman's Creek. They hurried through the dark, raising clouds of dust, laughing until they reached the sign that said OAK GROVE. HOME SWEET HOME.

Martha stared at the words. Her throat and eyes felt hot, as if this silly sign could make her cry.

"Which way?" Eel said softly in the dark.

The moon was behind a cloud, and Martha and Trout felt tentative as well. They were both thinking of people who'd disappeared and were never found again, and of how hard it was to leave behind the people you loved, even if the life you wanted wasn't the one they could give you.

Trout took out the compass, then pointed down the road. "East to the ocean. We just keep going."

They told themselves they weren't runaways,

they were run-tos. But running is running either way. After a while, they all felt as though they had eaten spoonfuls of lead, and that made running even more difficult. After the first mile they had the shivers. A mile more and they had the shakes. Oak Grove seemed very far away, and when they walked through the woods they could hear things moving. Owls and shrews, bobcats and raccoons. Deer so startled to see the three friends cutting across the meadows, they froze in place.

When Martha's feet began to hurt and the boys' eyes grew blurry, they stopped to make camp beneath a twisted oak tree, one of the oldest in the county. Tomorrow, school would start at exactly eight-thirty, but they wouldn't be in attendance. If they hadn't had other concerns they might have begun to worry about what people would think when they didn't show up for their classes, but for now, all they could concentrate on was their growling stomachs. Martha unpacked the food she had brought along, and Eel produced a Thermos, although too much salt had been added to the water for Martha to take more than a sip.

In the moonlight the McGill brothers' complexions turned faintly blue, and the webbing between their fingers was iridescent.

"What's the matter?" Trout asked when he caught Martha staring. "Afraid you're out here with freaks?"

"I'm out here with my two best friends," Martha said.

Trout looked at her with so much gratitude,

Martha knew they would be friends forever, no matter what their final destination might be.

Eel was exhausted, but ever since he'd lost his seashell he'd had trouble getting to sleep. He needed a story, the comforting babble of voices like waves on the shore. "Tell me about when you danced with your mother," he said to Martha.

"We'd go outside when everyone else in town was sleeping," Martha told him, even though she'd told him this story many times before. "She always wore her yellow shawl."

Martha reached into her backpack and brought out the shrunken shawl, and the boys understood that even though she was running to something, she was also running away.

"You can still wear it," Trout told her. "You can dance right here. Right now."

But there were no stars in the sky, and Martha shook her head. Her face was cloudy. "I don't know if I remember the dances. I'm afraid that before long I won't remember her, either."

"We don't remember our first mother," Eel said. The boys rarely spoke of their lives before they'd come to Oak Grove.

"I remember," Trout said. "Or at least, some things. I remember that she liked to swim, and when she laughed it sounded like a waterfall."

They were so tired, they fell asleep without trying. They were still far from the ocean, but Trout dreamed the same dream he had every night. He was on a beach, and before him the water was dark. A storm was coming up, just like Charlie McGill always feared, and out in the waves, someone was hurt and going under. Someone was calling to him. *Swim,* she was saying. *Swim to the land.*

Where Eel slept, in a tangle of leaves, he had the very same dream as his brother, but he didn't know it. Because he was younger he didn't remember as much, awake or in his dreams. All he saw were the blue waves. Whoever was calling was so far out to sea, he couldn't make out her face. The blue of everything was filling up his eyes, and his heart, and everything he had ever known.

Martha had a different dream entirely. In

her dream she was on a street that was made of sugar, and every time she tried to dance, she slipped and there was no one beside her to break her fall. Martha lurched out of sleep, still feeling as though she were falling. It was morning, but the sky was gray and thick with storm clouds. This was definitely not good weather for running to anything. Up above, the branches of the old oak were shaking, harder and harder still. One of the branches groaned as it broke. Before Martha could move away, it crashed onto her arm.

Without thinking, she called out for her mother. Trout hurried over and hauled the branch off. He asked Martha if she could move her arm, but it hurt too much to try.

"This isn't good," Trout said.

"It will be fine," Martha insisted, but she didn't sound very sure of herself, and when she sat up the pain made her gasp. She could tell from the expression in Trout's eyes that the dream of the ocean was fading, and she didn't want to be the reason for a loss like that. "I mean it will be fine," she insisted. "And I'm not going back, if that's what you're thinking."

"You have to see Dr. Marsh," Trout told her. "I'm pretty certain it's broken."

The wind was so wild, they had to shout just to hear each other.

"This isn't your fault," Trout hollered. "We just picked the wrong day to leave. I've never seen weather like this."

True enough, Oak Grove hadn't had more than morning dew for years, and now the sky was swirling and Martha's arm was throbbing. All the same, even if she had to go back, she didn't have to ruin everything. "You should go on without me."

"Maybe I should," Trout said. "I just don't want to."

When Martha heard this, she smiled in spite of the pain she felt. Trout McGill would never abandon his best friend. For the first time in ages, Martha felt happy, even though her arm ached.

They woke Eel, who lurched to his feet, arms flailing, as though he'd been drowning in his sleep. When they explained they had to turn back, Eel didn't argue, and a part of him, the part that was worried about Charlie and Kate McGills' hearts being broken when they opened the brothers' bedroom door and found them gone, was relieved.

The weather was more threatening by the minute. Rabbits ran into the hollows. Blackbirds tried to hide in the thickets. Thunder echoed and came closer. Soon enough, the first big drops began to fall. It was the sort of rain that was cold and nasty and fell in sheets, as though a spigot had been turned on up in the sky. Martha was chilled to the bone. The boys, however, weren't bothered in the least by the rain. They drank in the drops and laughed as their clothes and shoes became soaked. Watching them, Martha felt she had never seen her friends happier. It was as if they'd been desperate for water all their lives.

In town, people woke up in fear, remembering the storm of the past. The wind had already blown away the note Martha had left for her father and torn the paper into tatters. That same wind whipped through one room after another as Kate and Charlie McGill searched for their sons. The bakery shut down for the first time in fifteen years, with a batch of cinnamon rolls still in the oven, for electricity and gas lines were knocked out by the strong gusts. Dogs huddled under tables and refused to go into their yards. Children stayed home from school. The sky looked the way an ocean does when a hurricane is near, with swells twenty feet tall, and wind mixing with water, and no mercy for those on land or at sea.

Martha and the McGill boys knew they had to hurry. The morning had turned as dark as night. The friends had never seen a sky so wild. Lightning split the horizon, and water poured down. When at last they reached the road, they saw that the gullies and ditches had filled and were beginning to overflow. Meadows were turning into lakes, and Penman's Creek was a rushing river whose waters were unable to drain because of the stone wall.

At first the water on the road was up to the friends' ankles; then it was up to their knees. They couldn't help but think of the old days they'd heard about, when all of Oak Grove was

submerged underwater and people lost everything they owned.

By now, the rain was so heavy, Martha could
barely see where she was going.

"Just follow the white line down the middle
of the road," Trout shouted over the wind, but
before long that line disappeared into the swirl
of murky water that was quickly reaching their
waists.

Eel took out his compass, and they tried
their best to head west, huddled together to pre-
vent the wind from buffeting Martha and her
aching arm. Just when they thought they had
journeyed in the wrong direction they came
upon the sign — OAK GROVE. HOME SWEET
HOME. Although it had all but vanished in
the rising waters, the sign was still the highest,

driest spot around. Martha took out her mother's shawl before she let the backpack float away. The three friends hurried to roost on the very top of the sign. From this perch they saw that all over Oak Grove people had climbed onto their rooftops and were clinging to their chimneys. Penman's Creek had overflowed, and the center of town was the hardest hit.

"This is horrible," Martha said, thinking of her father having to bail out their basement and the grocery store. She noticed the brothers were grinning. "What is it?" she demanded. "What's so funny?"

"It looks like the way we pictured the ocean," Trout told her.

The rain had slowed to a mere pitter-patter, and they realized that what they heard now were the floodwaters washing back and forth like a tide.

"Listen," Eel said. It was just like the echo inside his shell. One wave after another. Water as far as the eye could see.

chapter
Three

By afternoon the sky had begun to turn blue, and the three friends had dried out on their perch above the sign. Trout had made a sling from Martha's mother's shawl to ensure that her arm would be protected from further harm until they got to Dr. Marsh's.

"We're still just as far away from the ocean as ever," Martha said. "There go your dreams."

"I'm starting to think that my dream is real," Trout said as he looked out over the water.

"I remember being in the ocean. I remember our mother tried to protect us when a speedboat came too close, and the propeller hit her."

Trout might have recalled more if they hadn't heard somebody shouting. "Save me!" a boy was screaming as he was dragged along what used to be downtown but what was now downstream. It was Richard Grady, who had so enjoyed calling the McGill brothers names. One minute Richard had been riding his bike, taunting the cats stuck up in trees and laughing at folks who were bailing out their basements, and the next minute Penman's Creek had overflowed and he'd been washed away. Like most of the children in this dry town he'd never learned how to swim. Now, Richard Grady held tight to his floating bicycle, thrashing and screaming, certain he was about to drown. "Help me!" he called to the friends on their perch.

Before Martha could call back that Richard had better ask nicely if he wanted their help, and apologize for every nasty word he'd ever said, Trout jumped into the water, cutting through the currents as though he were indeed related to his namesake. He grabbed Richard by his sleeve before he was washed into even deeper waters, and Eel jumped in after his brother to help haul Richard to the safety of the Oak Grove sign. When Richard climbed up, the sign shook under his weight, and Martha had to hold on tight with her good arm.

"A thank-you would be in order," Martha

advised as Richard Grady wiped the water out of his eyes.

"Oh, yeah. Sure. Thanks." Richard was still in shock by how quickly the world had shifted. Six feet of water where before there had been none, and those he least expected to save him becoming his rescuers.

"I hope you regret calling the McGills all those horrid names," Martha said.

"I don't know about that." Richard peered into the water. "I still don't think they're exactly normal. You may have noticed, they're not coming up for air."

Martha saw that indeed Trout and Eel had disappeared in the murky water. The oddest things were floating by — flowerpots and trash cans, doghouses and mailboxes — but there wasn't a glimpse of the boys.

Martha grabbed Richard by the collar of his soaking shirt. "Where did they go?" she demanded, her voice shaking.

"Under the water." Richard seemed a little afraid of how upset Martha was. "I swear they were there one minute and gone the next."

Martha jumped down from the sign to find that the water was now much too deep to stand. She took a deep breath and went under, straining to keep her eyes open, frantically searching for her friends. She worried about what tragic and watery scene might greet her, but there the boys were, swimming underwater, having the time of their lives.

When they caught sight of Martha, they waved, but Martha couldn't wave back. She had lost her balance and been pulled into a whirlpool, a spinning circle of wild water right at the corner of Elm Street, where Penman's Creek ran into the gutters.

With only one strong arm, it was impossible for Martha to break free of the whirlpool. She felt herself going down, and she saw a bit of her life race before her eyes — her father's kind face, the yellow stars of a summer night, her mother's cool hands when Martha was little and suffering from a fever. Maybe these images helped her to think fast. Before she could be carried away, Martha pulled off the sling that had been made of her mother's shawl and lassoed one of the posts of the Oak Grove sign.

The silk shawl was surprisingly strong; not even the whirlpool could take Martha away.

It took only a few seconds for the McGill boys to swim to Martha. One blink and they were there, helping her into calmer waters.

"Are you okay?" Trout asked.

Despite the pain in her arm and a tight feeling in her chest, Martha nodded. She had let go of the shawl when the McGill boys pulled her to safety, and it hung on the sign like a banner before the waters washed it away. Martha felt tears sting her eyes.

"Boy oh boy, I thought you were a goner," Richard Grady called to Martha from his perch.

"Then why didn't you help?" Martha called back. As the McGill brothers guided Martha onto the only high ground left, a stretch that ran parallel to Main Street that had been a hill before the flood, Martha thought about how comfortable Trout and Eel had seemed underwater. They'd looked as though they were somewhere they finally belonged.

From high on the hill the friends had an even better view of town. They could hear people shouting and calling for help. Even Richard Grady, now alone on the sign, was worried.

"My father said the water will keep rising until the wall at the creek is taken down," he said. "Then the water could flow out of town the way it used to."

Trout and Eel looked at each other. Even though they knew it had taken Charlie McGill and his crew two weeks to build the wall, Martha could tell what the McGill boys had in mind. She would have helped if she could, but it was clear she could never keep up with her friends, not even if she had the use of both of her arms.

"Good luck," she cried as the boys dove into the water.

Someone was calling her name, and Martha looked to see Jeanette Morton from the bakery stuck on the other side of the hill. Jeanette was sitting on the roof of her car eating cinnamon rolls. Martha sloshed over, and Jeanette helped her up. Martha was so hungry, she ate two of the delicious pastries before she answered Jeanette's question of what had happened to her arm.

"Possibly broken," Martha said between mouthfuls.

"My goodness!" Jeanette said. "And what do the McGill boys think they're doing? That water is dangerous."

"They'll be fine," Martha said, trying to convince herself of their safety as well. After all, she had seen how they swam underwater, their webbed hands flashing like flippers.

"What about your father? Is he all right?" Jeanette had an expression that was both worried and faraway. She had been a good friend of Martha's mother, but ever since Hildy had entered the picture, she hadn't come around.

"I'm sure Hildy's taking care of him," Martha reminded her.

"Oh, Hildy," Jeanette said sadly.

"Oak Grove is filled with awful things and terrible people," Martha said. "I'm like my mother when it comes to this town. I belong in a city, like New York or Paris or San Francisco. I'm leaving as soon as I can."

"But your mother loved Oak Grove. She told me the happiest day of her life was when she came here and met your father. She used to go out in the field beyond Penman's Creek at night and dance before you were born." Jeanette smiled at the memory. "I went with her sometimes. I never saw anything as beautiful."

Before Martha had time to think this over, a rowboat appeared on the flooded road. There were her father and Charlie McGill, paddling down the center of Main Street.

"Ahoy!" Jeanette Morton called, waving both hands above her head.

"Jeanette, you're a peach. You rescued my daughter," Mr. Glimmer called, and Martha didn't bother to correct her father. She didn't let him know she hadn't needed rescuing, because she saw the way Jeanette Morton was beaming. Martha couldn't help but wish that Jeanette had been the one who had started bringing over casseroles.

"Thank goodness you're safe," Mr. Glimmer said to Martha as he helped her into the rowboat. Martha winced, and her father realized she'd been hurt. "I'm taking you right to Dr. Marsh's."

He hugged Martha, and she felt truly happy in spite of her arm and her waterlogged clothes.

Her father seemed back to his old self, and she almost let out a whoop of joy. But then she noticed Mr. McGill. He was green and sorrowful, like a seasick man.

"My boys," Mr. McGill moaned. "Where have they gone?"

It took one look to know he was afraid that he and Mrs. McGill had lost those they loved most in this world.

"Don't worry," Martha told him. "They're the best swimmers you ever saw. They can outswim anyone."

Charlie McGill shook his head. He didn't try to hide the fact that there were big, salty tears in his eyes.

"That's exactly what I was afraid of," he said.

chapter
four

Ten years earlier Charlie and Kate McGill had gone on vacation to Ocean City at just about this time of year. Though they believed they were meant to be someone's parents, they never had been and this made even the happiest times a little less happy for them. Charlie McGill always said, *What happens is what's meant to be,* and Kate McGill always nodded and said, *I suppose that's true,* but she often had a wistful look on her face, even on vacation.

The McGills went to the boardwalk and ate ice cream, and in the evenings they strolled along the beach. Their life together wasn't what they had expected, but even without a house full of children, they could still enjoy their holiday. Kate and Charlie McGill might have gone back home to Oak Grove as they did every year, back to their quiet, childless lives, if they hadn't gone walking on the beach one windy night.

They hadn't even noticed how far they'd gone until the rain began. The storm surprised them, and they found themselves stranded on a stretch of sand with waves crashing all around. There was an abandoned fisherman's shack on the beach, once owned by a sailor who'd drowned in a storm such as this, and Charlie and Kate McGill would have made a run for it and sat out the bad weather if Charlie hadn't heard a woman's cries.

She was out where the shore was riddled with rocks, where the strongest currents had been known to pull down even the most experienced sailors. All the same, Charlie told his wife he had no choice. He had to help whoever was calling from beyond the waves. He swam as hard as he could, fighting the storm and the tides, but he stopped and treaded water when he saw what had happened. A beautiful woman with long, pale hair had been gouged by the propeller of a speedboat hurrying back to the marina; whoever had captained the speedboat had been unaware of anything out in front of him other than crashing waves.

The woman's skin was iridescent, and the

blood that washed into the waves and floated on the surface of the water appeared to be blue. Her strength was gone, and she was going under; she might have already given up and sunk to the depths if she hadn't had two little boys with her. Her fight to survive was strong, but she clearly couldn't hold on much longer.

Please, she said to Charlie McGill. *Take them.* She spoke slowly, for she'd learned only bits of English from the sailor she had loved, the one who had drowned in the last storm.

Charlie McGill ferried the boys to shore, struggling against the sea, then went right back into the water to rescue their mother. By then, all he could see was the flash of a dark blue tail as she helplessly disappeared. But there, floating on a bed of seaweed, the mermaid had left something behind for her children: two beautiful rings. One was a circle of abalone shell, and one a circle of oyster shell.

Charlie McGill took the rings and swam back to shore. On that evening, Charlie and Kate made a vow to keep the boys away from the water and to care for them all of their lives. Storms had taken both of the boys' natural parents, and the sea was always unpredictable. But try as you might to protect people from danger, you cannot keep them from their true nature.

"A mermaid's last wish is always for her children to swim free," Charlie McGill now told Martha, "but these boys also belong to the land."

Hearing this story, Martha was torn. She wanted freedom and safety both for her friends. She decided that the best she could ever hope for was that the McGill boys be granted what they longed for most of all.

By now, Trout and Eel had reached the rock wall that held back the waters. Trout had been timing himself and had found he could hold his breath underwater for more than ten minutes. This was humanly impossible, and he knew it.

"When you dream about our mother," Eel asked, "does she have webbing between her fingers, too?"

"She does," Trout said.

"And between her toes?"

Trout's memory had come back in waves, helped along by the storm. The way she taught them to dive. The way she combed her hair with a shell. "No toes. She had a tail, like a fish."

Eel thought this over as they swam along. The cold water felt good on his skin. He had never had a swimming lesson in his life, and yet, like his brother, in the water he was faster and stronger than any champion. "But we don't have tails."

"Maybe we've lived on land too long, or maybe we're half regular old human. But we're half of whatever she was, too."

The boys had kicked off their shoes, and the webbing between their toes gave them the streamlined glide of a porpoise. Quick as could be, they examined the stone wall that had been built to keep water out of Oak Grove and now had to be taken down to allow the floodwaters to drain. Trout knew what he had to do.

"All I need to do is pull the biggest rock out of the wall, and the rest will tumble down."

Now that Trout understood who he really was, his green eyes were luminous. With his wet hair slicked back, he seemed more like himself. Still, he remembered that even a mermaid could have a terrible accident and drown, and he didn't want his little brother to take any chances. "Stay here," he told Eel. "Don't follow me."

Trout disappeared in the direction of the wall of stones that Charlie McGill had constructed years ago. Eel paddled around nervously. He would do anything for his brother, except this. He couldn't let Trout go on alone, so he dove underwater as well.

Eel could see surprisingly far in the muddy water. There was Trout wrestling with the largest rock in the wall. It looked as if it should have been immovable, but after a moment it creaked and tipped. Quite suddenly, it fell, dragging Trout along with it. There was a landslide of stones, and it all happened so fast, Trout hadn't time to get away.

Eel wasn't strong enough to lift the heavy stones off his brother, and yet he did. People find strength they never knew they had at certain times, and this was one of them. The brothers nodded to each other, green eye to green eye. Eel used all the strength of the seas as he pulled off the stones, freeing his brother. Together, they swam to the surface, darting away from the rushing waters that could now flow out of town.

The river that Main Street had become began to drain, with wild currents and whirlpools everywhere. People on their roofs called out their approval. They cheered from whatever high ground they'd managed to find as the waters receded from basements and kitchens and roadsides alike.

One rowboat sat bobbing in the ebbing waters like an apple in a tub. Charlie McGill stood up the moment he saw the boys swimming toward him. He waved his arms and called, and if Martha and her father hadn't taken hold of his jacket, Charlie might have jumped into the water to meet Trout and Eel.

The brothers towed the rowboat to what was not quite dry land, a muddy place they recognized as the school soccer field.

Martha jumped from the boat and hugged her friends, one after the other, with her good arm. "You saved everyone," she told them.

Mr. Glimmer shook the boys' hands and patted their backs. But it was Charlie McGill the boys were worried about, and it was to him they turned.

"Good work," Charlie said.

He had never in his life been prouder than he was right now. Trout and Eel threw their muddy arms around their father.

"I thought if you got too near to water, you would swim away," Charlie said as he held the boys close.

"We will," Trout said.

"But then we'll swim back," Eel added. "We're your sons. You can never lose us."

When the McGills got back to their muddy house, Kate McGill was waiting at the door. Kate had made a vow to take care of these boys from the day they were found in the sea, and she'd remained true to her promise. She loved them as if she were their natural mother, but there was someone else who had loved them, too. For all these years Kate McGill had been waiting to give the boys a special gift, one she'd kept stored in a box fashioned out of starfish and shells that she'd bought long ago in Ocean City. She gave Eel the ring made of abalone shell, and Trout the ring made of oyster shell, and that's when they knew they were home.

chapter
five

Dr. Marsh set Martha's broken arm that evening. His office was filled with weary, damp people who had turned their ankles in the mud or sprained their backs toting buckets of water out of their basements. Dr. Marsh assured Martha that she'd soon be able to throw rocks at tin cans again, but for now she had best take it easy. Afterward, Martha and her father walked home. They waved to their neighbors, who all agreed that a clear, starry night had never looked better. Even Martha admitted that Oak Grove seemed brand new, as if the floodwaters had washed everything clean.

"I thought you had it in your head to leave Oak Grove," Mr. Glimmer said.

"I might," Martha told him. "Someday. But not now. When I grow up. I'll travel and see all the places where my mother used to live, but today I'll go home, and wash all this mud off, and be polite to Hildy Swoon, because that's what you want me to do."

"I don't think that will be necessary," Mr. Glimmer said. "When the storm came up, Hildy hightailed it to her mother's house up on the mountain. I don't think she'll be coming back. She's happier having things her own way."

Unless Martha was mistaken, her father looked almost as pleased as she was by this news. Martha wanted to do a little dance, but instead she only nodded.

"Sometimes people get so lonely, they don't know what to do," Mr. Glimmer said, and Martha knew exactly what he meant. When her mother was sick, Martha often went into the yard and danced under the stars until she was too dizzy to feel anything. Now, whenever she looked at the night sky, she was reminded of her mother and she felt good and lonely all mixed up together.

"Maybe we should invite Jeanette Morton over sometime," Martha said. "She's lonely, too."

While Mr. Glimmer thought this over, he took the yellow shawl from his pocket. "I found this floating by. I knew you'd want it."

Martha hugged her father and gratefully took the shawl. After they'd cleaned the water and muck out of their house, she washed the shawl and dried it carefully. For years to come she would carry it with her whenever she danced. Her feet already felt lighter.

That night she went into the yard. With the yellow shawl held high, she danced beneath the stars once more. She danced until she was so dizzy she could feel everything, especially the way she missed her mother.

The McGills stayed in town until the end of the school term. They didn't decide to leave because people made fun of the brothers or because they didn't fit in. Far from it. Everyone was grateful that the boys had broken through the seawall. This summer, people would go swimming in the refilled Penman's Creek, and every time they did they would be thankful to the McGill brothers. As for Richard Grady, he soon taught himself how to swim and began to give lessons to the younger children, who gave him the nickname of Fin, a name he was proud to possess in honor of the boys who'd saved him from the flood.

The reason Charlie and Kate McGill had decided to move was because they truly understood that the boys belonged as much to the water as to the land, and because it was what Trout had always wished for — to see the ocean. The McGills sold their house and the construction company and bought a place near the cove where the fisherman had lived, where they'd found the boys.

"It doesn't seem fair," Trout said to Martha on the boys' last night in town. They were up on the garage roof, just the two of them, for Eel was home packing. They weren't bothering to throw stones anymore. "I get my wish, and you don't."

Someday when Trout was all grown up, and she was, too, Martha might dance for him. Her father had agreed that she could take classes in the next town, where there was a dance school. And besides, Trout was wrong about Martha not getting her wish. Hildy Swoon was gone, after all, and Oak Grove didn't look so bad anymore.

The truth was, it looked like home.

"Now that you remember your mother, do you miss her more?" Martha asked.

"I missed her, anyway," Trout said. "Now I just know who I'm missing."

On the day the McGills left town, Martha stood on the roof of the garage so that Trout and Eel could see her waving good-bye as they drove past. Even though her best friends were leaving, Martha felt lucky. She closed her eyes and wished them a good trip. She wished them everything they wished for themselves.

The McGills drove straight through to Ocean City. Finding the way was easy, straight over the mountains to a place they'd all been before. They reached the shore by suppertime, and as she was having her dinner with her father, Martha Glimmer could have sworn she, too, could hear the sound of the tides, an echo from the farthest sea, so deep and so blue, someone who had been there would never forget.